Frog in the HOUSe

To Lauren,

HOPPY READING!

Stephanie Mirocha
2013

By David Mather

Illustrated by Stephanie Mirocha

Raven Productions, Inc.
Ely, Minnesota

Text © 2011 by David Mather
Illustrations © 2011 by Stephanie Mirocha

Published September 2011 by
Raven Productions, Inc.
P.O. Box 188, Ely, MN 55731
218-365-3375
www.ravenwords.com
Printed in Minnesota

Stephanie Mirocha is a 2011 recipient of a Career Development grant from the Arrowhead Regional Arts Council, which is funded in part with money from the Minnesota Arts and Cultural Heritage Fund, appropriations from the Minnesota State Legislature, and funding from the McKnight Foundation.

Library of Congress Cataloging-in-Publication Data

Mather, David (David J.)
Frog in the house / by David Mather ; illustrated by Stephanie Mirocha.   p. cm.
Summary: A tree frog takes up residence in a potted tree on a family's porch, but when winter comes and the plant is brought inside, the frog cannot find food or a place to hibernate. Includes facts about tree frogs.
ISBN 978-0-9819307-8-7 (trade pbk. : alk. paper) --
ISBN 978-0-9819307-9-4 (hardcover library binding : alk. paper)
1. Hylidae--Juvenile fiction. [1. Tree frogs--Fiction.
2. Frogs--Fiction.] I. Mirocha, Stephanie, ill. II. Title.
 PZ10.3.M4198Fr 2011
 [E]--dc22   2011010196

United States of America
Corporate Graphics, N. Mankato, MN
10 9 8 7 6 5 4 3 2 1   072011

This book is for my daughter, Isabel, and my wife, Elizabeth. Isa, thank you for asking me to write the story of froggy's adventure. – DM

For my nephew, Jasper, and frog lovers everywhere.
– SM

For sharing their knowledge of treefrogs so that this book can be as scientifically accurate as current understanding permits, we appreciate: Mark Bee and Sandra Tekmen, Animal Communications Lab, University of Minnesota; Jim Cummings, Mille Lacs Kathio State Park; Carol Hall, Minnesota Department of Natural Resources; and John Moriarty, Ramsey County Parks.

A man made a little pond in his yard. He put me in there. I hopped out when he wasn't looking. He didn't look at my toes. I'm a *treefrog*!

I was born in the water, but I don't live there now. There are some nice bushes across the yard. I'll climb into them. I can hear the frogs that live across the street in the trees along the river bluff.

Up, up, I climb.

I've never seen a tree like this. It's not growing in the ground. It's in a pot. The porch is sort of like a forest. I climb my new tree. I'm hungry.

There's a caterpillar! Mmmmm… GULP!

I'm hiding. There are people right here! Water pours over me.

"Mommy, why do we water the plants on the porch?" asks a little girl. "Because there's a roof. The rain can't reach in here."

The nights are calm.
Bats fly by catching mosquitoes.
An owl hoots. Insects are buzzing.
Some of the moths and bugs
hover in my plants,
so I eat them up.

I sing along with the other frogs in the neighborhood.

One night is not calm. There are colored lights
in the sky, and loud booms and whistles.
Lots of people sit on my porch.
"Purple, green, red, blue! I like the red ones best!"
says the little girl.
"I do too," says the daddy. "Happy Fourth of July,
my sweetheart."

I still hide when the people are here,
but they're not so scary now.
I peek out to watch the little girl play.

I like the strange plants.
I find lots to eat here.
The little girl and her mommy
keep my home nice and damp.

The days are getting shorter.
The nights are cooler.
It makes me sleepy.
The pot at the bottom of my
tree has bark chips and leaves.
I can crawl under there when
the time comes.

The world is shaking!
What's going on?
I hold on tight to my tree.
The mommy is carrying it.
She puts it down *inside* the house!

She brings in the other
plants too. Now the house
is like a little forest.

Life is strange here. Sometimes there is music. The television makes noise and flashes colored lights. I don't hear other frogs. There are no birds singing and only a few flies buzzing.

I call to other frogs, but no one answers.
I try another time, and the people
gather around.
"What was that?" asks the daddy.
"It sounded like a robot chicken,"
says the mommy.
I decide to stay quiet.
They can't find me.

Days go by.
There are fewer and fewer bugs,
so I start hunting farther from
my tree. I feel like I should be
sleeping for the winter, but it's
not cold here. There is light at
strange times, but not from the
sun or moon.

I am so hungry.
Where are all the bugs?

"Where did you come from?"
says a voice. It's the daddy.
He sees me! I hop away
under toys and books.
I hide back in the plants.

"Froggy, froggy!" The little girl finds me
while I'm hunting for food in a tiny house.
"Will you play with me?"
I like her, but I'm shy. I don't know how
to play people games. I hop away fast.

Later the little girl shows her daddy how to hop like a frog. She does a good job.

It's nighttime and I'm hunting.
Suddenly it's light! I try to hide.

The mommy shows the little girl how to
hold me gently.
"This is a treefrog," says the daddy. "Let's put
froggy under the oak tree out back."
The little girl cries. "But I want the froggy
to be my friend."

Oh, sweet girl, I've always been your friend,
ever since I first saw you on the porch.
I wish I could play with you, but I don't know how,
and I'm so sleepy.

"The treefrog needs to hibernate,
to dig under the leaves and sleep
for the winter," says the mommy.
"A frog can't do that in the house.
It's too warm," says the daddy.
"Let's say good night now."
"Will I see froggy in the spring?"
asks the little girl bravely.
"I'm sure you will," says the daddy.
"Next spring we'll listen for the treefrog song."

Yes, my friends, look for me again.
I'll be singing for you.

What if you meet a treefrog?

A biologist was digging under a tree on a cold autumn day when he found a rock shaped like a frog. He put it in his pocket thinking that the frog-rock would be a decoration for his office. He shivered in the cold and went inside for a break. As he warmed up, he looked at the frog-rock again and found it was melting. Not only was it melting, it was soft. It wasn't a rock after all. It was a real frog, and it was alive!

Because of that discovery, we now know that some frogs survive the winter by freezing solid. They burrow below the fallen leaves. When the temperature drops below freezing, ice crystals form inside their bodies. A human couldn't survive this, but a frog just sleeps until spring.

The frog in this story is a gray treefrog. Scientists know this animal by its Latin name, *Hyla versicolor*. This taxonomic name is more accurate because the frog is not always gray. Its skin changes from shades of gray to green. *Hyla* means tree or wood. *Versicolor* means changing color.

Treefrogs are amphibians. Like most amphibians, they hatch from eggs in the water. Gray treefrogs develop into tadpoles–little round creatures with a tail for swimming, a high fin that extends from the tail up onto its back, and gills for breathing like a fish. Eventually the tadpole sprouts legs, the tail and fin go away, and the frog lives most of its life on land breathing air with lungs. Gray treefrogs are often found on backyard trees and bushes and even in potted plants.

Gray treefrogs go to ponds in the spring, when it's time to breed. The male frogs call to attract the females. The frog in this story was singing, so we know it was a male. It is unusual that it called in the autumn, although this sometimes happens.

You can look for tadpoles in ponds, slow-moving creeks, and along quiet lakeshores. The best way to see a treefrog is to find it when it is singing. You have to be patient and look carefully because its color provides good camouflage.

Gray treefrogs will climb up to thirty feet above the ground. Considering that they are only about two inches long, this would be like you climbing up the side of a skyscraper. Don't try this at home!

If you handle a tadpole or frog, wash and rinse your hands before and after. This protects both you and the frog. Amphibians have permeable skin, which means that water and pollutants can easily pass through. If you have soap, bug repellent, other chemicals, or germs on your hands they could make the frog sick.

This story ended when the frog still had time to hibernate outside. Like other wild animals, treefrogs don't make good pets. But what would you do if you found one in your house in the winter, after the ground was frozen? You could try to feed it insects and then release it in the spring. Contact a local herpetologist (a scientist who studies reptiles and amphibians) for advice. Staff at a nearby park, museum, university, or zoo can direct you to the right person.